By

Christine Conrad Cazes

Illustrations by Kalpart

Strategic Book Publishing and Rights Co.

Strategic Book Publishing and Rights Co., LLC
USA | Singapore
www.sbpra.com

For information about special discounts for bulk purchases, please contact Strategic Book Publishing and Rights Co., LLC. Special Sales, at bookorder@sbpra.net.

ISBN: 978-1-946540-50-8

To my little granddaughter, Julia, who enjoys opening the pages of a good book and listening to my stories.

Dew moistened the freshly plowed pasture. Daylight broke, erasing the shadows that draped the tiny green pumpkin huddled in the eastern orchard of Westorchid, where only the finest pumpkins grew.

Soon I'll be large enough and they'll select me for the Halloween Harvest Fair, thought the young pumpkin.

As the days passed, the green seedling felt his roots extend beyond the ground. With nourishment from the rain and sun, he could feel his body growing larger and he could see his mint green color starting to fade.

"If I continue to grow at this rate," cried the pumpkin, "I'll be the biggest and the best pumpkin in this patch!"

All day long, the pumpkin bathed in the sun or drank the rain and chatted to himself. Soon, birds began to whisper and sing songs to the tiny pumpkin.

"Music is good for the soul," chirped the young sparrow. "My music will help you grow,

P-u...P-u..." she struggled to pronounce his name. "P-u-n-kin!" she named him.

The little pumpkin blinked in approval at the sound of his new name. He giggled, "Music! Good! Sing more! I want to grow big! I want to be selected for the Halloween Harvest. Everyone tells me it's a wonderful event."

"Wonderful, indeed!" chimed the older wren in a hoarse voice. "I've seen hundreds of people staring at the pumpkins, and they offer a prize for the best design," she continued, perching herself on Punkin's head.

"Design?" questioned Punkin. "What design?"

"Ah!" continued the wren while fluffing her feathers. "They carve wonderful faces on the pumpkins. They become cats and owls or witches and goblins. Some are funny. Others are frightening. It's spectacular! Everyone loves it!"

"I want to know more about the Harvest!" cried Punkin. "It sounds like a wonderful chance to make everyone happy. Could anyone tell me more about this day?"

The nosey hare jumped out of her hole. "When I hopped up to the Halloween Harvest," exclaimed the excited long-eared rabbit, "I saw many people dressed in costumes carrying bundles of candy. There were scarecrows and stacks of straw snuggled around huge tables filled with cookies and pies and apple cider that quenched everyone's thirst. Everyone laughed and giggled and paraded around in a circle displaying their costumes."

"It sounds wonderful," said the enthusiastic Punkin.

"It's fantastic!" interrupted the fawn. She was hidden behind the apple tree listening to their conversation. "When I peeped my nose through the trees," she said in a small, quiet voice, "I saw candles glowing from the pumpkins. They were magical!"

Punkin listened to these wonderful stories and prayed that he would grow large enough to be selected for this wonderful October event.

Weeks passed and finally a hint of orange appeared on his forehead. "Nice color," remarked the sparrow as she flew around his head. "You're bound to be selected for the Harvest Fair!"

"I hope so," replied Punkin. "But yesterday, I noticed that there were other pumpkins in the patch who were much larger than me. I want to be selected, but my color needs to be brighter and my shape rounder."

"Don't worry!" consoled the hare. "Rain is expected and mother assured me that the sun wouldn't get too hot in the days to follow."

"Perfect!" replied Punkin. "I need rain and sunshine to grow into the largest pumpkin in this patch!"

Rain eventually trickled down beneath the soil and fed the pumpkin's roots. Sunlight nourished his body and the little pumpkin grew larger and larger and larger.

A few weeks later, an old rickety wooden truck pulled into the pumpkin patch. Everyone could hear it CRUNCH and CREAK as it traveled down the field, stopping and starting, to gather pumpkins.

"IT'S HARVEST TIME!" cried Punkin. "But I'm so hidden on this small acre. I don't have a chance! They don't even see me here!" he whimpered to himself as the wooden truck filled with pumpkins left without him. The next day, the wheels creaked down the road again and Punkin recognized the sound. "They're here again!" he cried. "I'M OVER HERE!" he shouted.

This time there were fewer pumpkins in the patch. Closer and closer the men approached. The sound of their steps caused Punkin to breathe hard as the truck approached his pumpkin patch. His heart almost burst when a large hand reached down and pulled him from the ground.

"I'VE BEEN CHOSEN!" screamed Punkin. "I'll be the best pumpkin at the Halloween Harvest! I know it!"

The Halloween Harvest Fair finally arrived. The festivities commenced and all the pumpkins sat patiently displaying their unique beauty. . . except Punkin. He fidgeted back and forth and wrinkled his nose.

Pick me! Pick me! I'm the best! he thought. The judges moved up and down the aisle examining each pumpkin.

"Here! Here I am! Here!" Punkin attempted shouting as the judges moved closer. Suddenly, they stopped in front of Punkin. He held his breath and sat perfectly still.

The judges stared and minutes seemed to turn into hours for Punkin until the judge announced, "That's it!"

His baritone voice broke the dead silence as he declared, "This pumpkin is the winner! It has the roundest body and the brightest orange color."

"IT'S ME!" shouted Punkin from the eastern orchard of Westorchid. "I'VE WON!"

The judges lifted Punkin above their heads and everyone nodded in agreement that he was the best pumpkin in the patch. Then, the once small pumpkin was placed upon a long black table that shimmered in the candlelight.

"How exciting!" exclaimed Punkin as he noticed the flickering lights cast shadows on the grand table where he sat proudly high above the ground. *I wonder what my new face will look like?* he thought.

Punkin stared into the dark night trying to remember all the Halloween designs described by his friend, Wren. Deep in thought, Punkin suddenly jumped. He was startled by the soft touch of a hand caressing his face. Quickly, he turned his head and gazed at the wavering image of a young woman dressed in a long, flowing, black gown. She gently wiped away the beaded drops of water that trickled down his forehead. Punkin enjoyed her gentle touch which assured him that he was the best pumpkin in the hidden eastern orchard of Westorchid.

The woman stood still admiring the beautiful round pumpkin who sat impatiently before her. At that moment, she bent down slowly to calm his nerves and whispered into his ear, "Close your eyes, Punkin, and *D R E A M!*" Her words drifted into the dusk's gentle breeze and she disappeared into the shadows of the night's festivities.

Blinking in disbelief, Punkin nodded and closed his eyes. As he listened to the enchanting sounds of the harvest's fall evening, his mind drew images of the faces that he remembered in his little orchard.

"Which one will be mine?" he whispered. Punkin felt dizzy with excitement.

Trying to keep his eyes closed, he felt a cool breeze touch his face. Breaths of air seeped through every crevice of his body and Punkin's face slowly began to change under the moonlight.

I hope everyone likes my new face! thought Punkin.

Punkin's face slowly began to look different as his round orange body transformed, revealing a broad happy grin with moon crescent eyes and a diamond shaped nose. Punkin heard the crowd cheer as they gazed upon his newly sculpted face turning him into the most magnificent jack o' lantern anyone had ever seen.

"Everyone loves my new face!" cried Punkin in an astonished voice. "I am the best! I'm the very best pumpkin in the Halloween Harvest!"

All through the night, people in costumes paraded in front of the best jack-o'-lantern at the Halloween Harvest. Candy overflowed in children's bags as they sang their favorite Halloween songs.

"This is so much fun!" cried Punkin. The night's festivities ran into the dawn. Finally, silence spread her veil across the land and everyone slept. . . even the pumpkin who used to live in the east orchard of Westorchid.

19

Dawn arrived. Punkin's garden friends snuck into the fair grounds to admire his new face. Hare, Sparrow, Wren, and Fawn stared at Punkin.

"You look very different," noted the hare with a surprise in his voice.

"The edges around your eyes are black!" observed fawn.

"And your plump body doesn't seem so full anymore," noted wren in her raspy voice.

"I'm just a little tired," explained Punkin. "I'll be better tonight for the festivities."

The hare hesitated and the sparrow chirped abruptly, "What festivity? There's no festivity this evening. Halloween is over!"

"Oh! I'm sure they'll do something special for me!" cried Punkin. "After all, I'm the best!"

22

But the days passed and no one approached the once beautiful pumpkin. Crows began to nibble on his cheeks and head while he closed his eyes and dreamed of the east orchard in Westorchid where the sun shone and rain fell bringing nourishment to all the pumpkins in the patch.

Punkin's smile soon disappeared. He couldn't talk. He couldn't grin. He was no longer plump and his bright orange color was now dark brown. Punkin could only close his eyes and see himself sitting in his orchard talking to the sparrow and laughing with hare, wren, and fawn. He dreamed of the Halloween Harvest and whispered to himself, "I was the best!"

Later, he opened his eyes and noted, "We were all the *BEST* in the eastern orchard of Westorchid." In a weak little voice he continued to say, "We were all the *best. . . best. . . best* in our pumpkin patch." His words faded and Punkin slowly withered to the ground. The wise wren perched upon her branch was listening to Punkin's lamenting words. She sang a song to her friend as he grew smaller and smaller before her eyes.

Punkin, sweet Punkin,

Let your tears of sorrow reach the sun

And crawl through the cloud's timeless tunnel.

Punkin, sweet Punkin,

Dream of the green meadow where coral

Pumpkins become young soldiers saluting freedom.

Punkin, sweet Punkin,

Remember the eastern orchard of Westorchid

Where every pumpkin is the best.

A tear trickled from Punkin's eye and he sighed his last breath, "I was the *best!*" 24

The wren watched quietly as her friend disappeared, leaving only a single pumpkin seed. With great precision, she spread her wings and flew down to Punkin. She placed his last seed in her beak and quickly flew away to that tiny orchard in Westorchid. She opened her beak and dropped Punkin's last seed on the hidden acre in the eastern orchard.

Falling through the air, the seed cried for everyone to hear, "I'm home."

CPSIA information can be obtained
at www.ICGtesting.com
Printed in the USA
BVOW05*1146311017
499162BV00001B/1/P

9 781946 540508